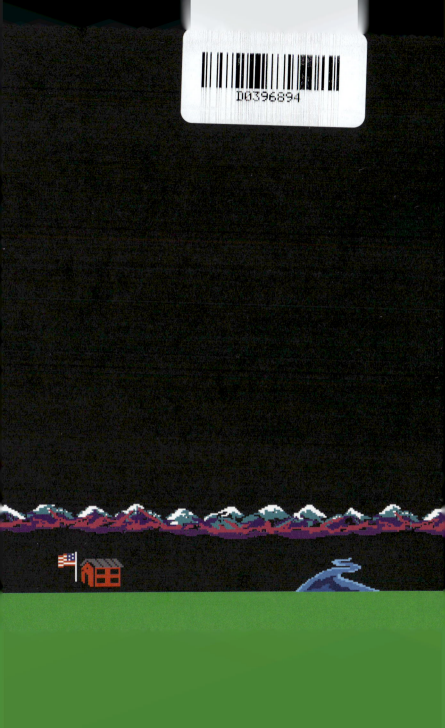

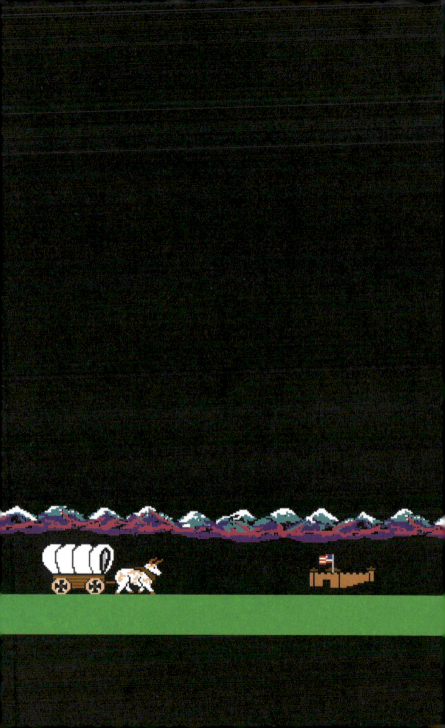

The Oregon Trail™

hmhco.com

The text was set in Garamond.
The display text was set in Pixel-Western, Press Start 2P, and Slim Thin Pixelettes.
Illustrations by June Brigman, Yancey Labat, Ron Wagner, Hi-Fi Color Design, and Walden Font Co.

ISBN: 978-1-328-55002-6 paper over board
ISBN: 978-1-328-54998-3 paperback

Printed in the United States of America
DOC 10 9 8 7 6 5 4 3 2 1
4500718770

The Oregon Trail™

3

THE SEARCH FOR SNAKE RIVER

by JESSE WILEY

Houghton Mifflin Harcourt
BOSTON   NEW YORK

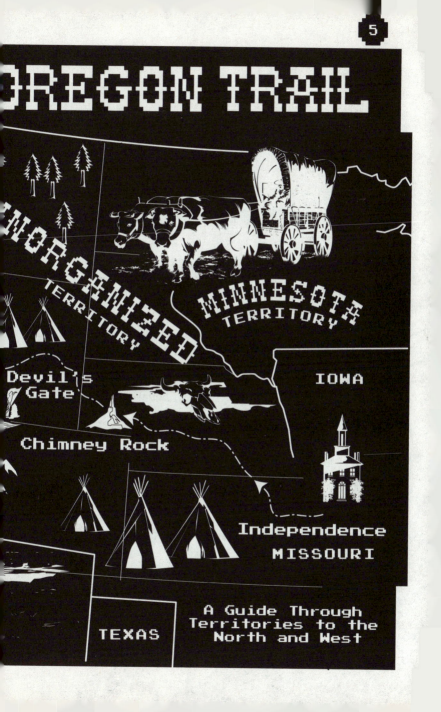

OREGON TRAIL

UNORGANIZED TERRITORY

MINNESOTA TERRITORY

Devil's Gate

IOWA

Chimney Rock

Independence

MISSOURI

TEXAS

A Guide Through Territories to the North and West

The Oregon Trail™

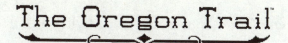

GO WEST
Explore the Frontier

You are a young pioneer headed West by wagon train in the year 1850. You and your family have already braved nearly half of the perilous frontier path known as the Oregon Trail, crossing 820 miles of territory in what will later become the states of Kansas, Nebraska, and Wyoming.

For fifteen miles a day for more than two months, you have walked beside your oxen and covered wagon. You can't ride in the wagon because it holds everything you need for the journey and for your family's new lives as farmers in Oregon.

You've crossed mountains, prairies, and rivers, and you've passed famous landmarks like Chimney Rock and Devil's Gate. You've also faced wild animals, stampeding buffalo, and learned to start a campfire with dried buffalo dung. You now know how to handle livestock and you've met members of the Cheyenne Nation, among other indigenous people. Best of all, there are still months of adventure ahead of you—*if* you can survive the dangerous ford of the wild Snake River at Three Island Crossing!

Only one path will lead you safely through the book to the Snake River, but there are twenty-three possible endings, full of risks and surprises. Along the way, no matter what path you choose, you will experience natural disasters, sickness, and other hazards of the Trail.

You're in a desert without water! What can you do?

A rattlesnake is ready to strike!

A forest fire roars nearby, how will you survive?

Before you begin, make sure to read the *Guide to the Trail* at the back of the book, starting on page 154. It's filled with important information you'll need to make wise choices.

You're not alone, and you'll get advice from friends, Native American people, or Ma and Pa—but sometimes it's best to trust your own good instincts. Make smart decisions and you'll find your way to Three Island Crossing!

Every second counts!
Think fast.
What will you do?

➜ Ready? ⬅

BLAZE A TRAIL TO

SNAKE RIVER!

☞

South Pass
JULY 13, 1850

Roll the wagons!" Caleb, your wagon train captain, commands. It's still early, but you scramble to help get your family's wagon moving with the rest of the train. Even though you've been on the Oregon Trail for over two months now, you're still impressed with how quickly everyone in your wagon train manages to finish morning chores, have breakfast, and repack the wagons before the starting bugle sounds. Then you set off on a full day's hike, which usually covers fifteen miles a day, though you've slowed down a little since entering the pass through the Rocky Mountains.

"When can we stop for lunch?" Samuel asks almost as soon as you start walking alongside your wagon.

You can't help but smile at him, even as you roll your eyes. Your little brother asks the same question every single day—and always just after breakfast.

"As soon as you see the sun touch those trees," Pa replies to Samuel, and points to the distance.

"Are we going to see anything interesting today?" your younger sister Hannah asks, tugging on Pa's sleeve.

You're curious about what landmarks are ahead, too. A week ago, your wagon train left Devil's Gate, a towering chasm cut right through the cliffs and the most remarkable sight of your journey so far. Plus, Caleb surprised you by taking you to a spot where you dug for ice, buried underneath the ground.

"Today we should reach South Pass," Pa says.

"It's the part of the trail where we finally enter into Oregon Territory," you say. "The Land of Promise!"

Ma looks at you with a wide smile. "We'll have finished half of our journey by then," she says.

Halfway at last! Your heart swells with pride that your family has made it this far. Ten weeks ago, you started your travels on the Trail in Independence, Missouri, after leaving your comfortable home in Kentucky in March. But then you sigh deeply as you realize that you still have an equally long way to go.

It's hard to imagine that this wide and gently sloping path is leading you through the Rocky Mountains. Pa tells you how the pass was discovered by fur traders over thirty years ago. Without the path, getting through the mountains would be impossible for the ten wagons that now make up your train.

"Here, boy," your friend Eliza calls out to Archie, your dog. Archie runs up to Eliza with his tail wagging. She hands him a morsel of bacon that she saved for him from breakfast.

Eliza and her brother, Joseph, Caleb's children, have become your best friends. Some of your favorite memories of this trip include the time spent exploring and playing games with them. And Archie has become really attached to Eliza, who takes the time to brush his coat after a long day's hike and always remembers to give him treats.

You walk for a few hours until it's time for "nooning," the midday rest everyone anticipates. Caleb had sent you, Joseph, and Eliza a little ways ahead of the wagons to help scout for a nice spot to rest. Ma likes the midday break because no one has to build a fire or cook anything. Instead, she pulls out leftovers from breakfast as a snack. You happily nibble on some cold flapjacks that were cooked in bacon grease, while the oxen rest and sip from the stream nearby.

"These are the Pacific Springs," Pa says. "We've left home waters behind."

"I'll drink to that," Caleb says, raising his water-skin with a grin. "From this point onward all waters flow into the Pacific Ocean instead of the Atlantic. We have just crossed the Continental Divide."

You take a moment to think about what that means. You've moved from the eastern part of the continent into the West. Amazing!

Hannah and Samuel take a nap in the wagon,

lying on their feather mats. You notice the soles of their sturdy walking shoes are almost completely worn out again after being repaired just a few weeks ago. Yours are in equally bad shape, and the rocky terrain ahead is only going to be rougher.

"We all need to make a very big decision in a couple days," you hear Caleb tell your folks. "We'll be reaching the Parting of the Ways."

You listen closely. With a name like that, you know it has to be important.

"At that point, there are two ways to go," Caleb continues. "We can continue on the Trail, or take the Greenwood Cutoff."

"What is the cutoff?" Ma asks.

"It's a shortcut that will take at least five or six days off our journey," Caleb explains. "But it will take us through a desert."

"How many miles of desert would we have to cross?" you ask.

"About fifty," Caleb explains.

"What's the other option?" Pa asks.

"We'd be heading south, toward Fort Bridger, and would have to cross the Green River," Caleb replies. "I've heard good and bad things about both options, so think about it."

For the next two days, all everyone talks about is the Parting of the Ways. When you finally approach the famous fork in the Trail, it is unmistakable. One set of wagon ruts leads to the left, toward Fort Bridger, while the other leads right, toward the cutoff. In the middle is a wooden pole. Plastered on it are scraps of paper with the names of those who have traveled through already, indicating which road each of them decided to take.

People in your group have strong opinions about which path is better. Some are convinced that saving a week with the cutoff is the only option that makes sense, even if it means crossing a desert. Others are frightened by the idea of a waterless journey and want to stick with the road to Fort Bridger, even if it means crossing the tricky Green River.

Pa turns to you to help decide which way to go. "What do you think we should do?" he asks.

If you say you should head to Fort Bridger,
turn to page **126**

If you say you should take the Greenwood Cutoff,
turn to page **106**

kay, let's run!" Joseph whispers, pulling you up by the hand. "Once they see us taking off toward our camp, they will probably leave us alone."

You start to move, hoping Joseph is right. The Shoshone people are still several yards away from you.

But suddenly you see Pa and Caleb approaching on horseback. They have found you!

Caleb brandishes his rifle. "Halt!" he shouts. You realize that he thinks you are in danger. But no one has done anything to you!

All the Shoshone people draw their bows and point arrows toward Pa and Caleb. Your heart is pounding as you realize this could start a battle. And Pa and Caleb are outnumbered.

"Hold on!" you shout, jumping in between them.

Joseph raises his arms. "We're okay, we're okay," he says breathlessly.

You see Pa look at you with a mixture of fear, anger, and relief. You feel a rush of guilt realizing how worried he must have been about you.

Caleb dismounts from his horse and walks slowly toward you. He's still holding his weapon, facing the drawn bows and arrows. Pa starts to get off his horse when an arrow zings through the air near his horse's neck.

"Whoa!" Pa cries. The horse startles and then takes off, with one of Pa's legs still in the stirrup.

"Pa!" you shout, as your father starts to get pulled along the ground. Caleb races after the horse on foot, trying to get it to stop. It finally does, but only after Pa has been dragged for several feet.

Caleb and a young Shoshone man help Pa down. You watch nervously as they lay Pa on the ground and carefully examine his injuries. Pa is unconscious and his leg is twisted in a way that it shouldn't be. It makes you want to throw up.

The Shoshone people end up taking all of you back to camp. They send a healer to help set Pa's leg straight and give him some medicine to help him. But it will be several months before Pa can walk again, and he's likely to limp for the rest of his life. In the meantime, he'll have to give up his dream, which has become your dream, too, of getting to Oregon.

 **THE END**

You're so upset about what happened to Gertrude that you agree to accept the gift from the Native American people. The animal skins won't bring your pet back, but they might come in handy for your family along the Trail. Maybe Ma can use them to make moccasins for your family when your shoes wear out completely. Your feet ache in your hard shoes, and the soles have worn thin, even though Pa repairs them with buckskins any chance he gets. The Lakota men bring you the skins, along with a beautiful woven blanket. They hand you the gifts, nod, and quickly leave. They seem kind, and, as they ride away on their horses, you wonder what type of relationship you might have had if you had tried to be friends.

You continue to travel toward Fort Bridger, plodding along as usual. But you start to feel more and more tired. Every day seems harder than the last. The walking for miles each day is almost unbearable.

One day, you try to sit in the wagon instead of walking. "What's the matter?" Pa asks.

"I'm not sure," you reply. "My legs are feeling really tired."

"Okay," Pa says. "Rest up as much as you can."

You know that sitting in the wagon just makes the trip harder on the oxen, but Pa looks at you with concern and lets you stay there longer than usual. That night, when you make camp, you don't feel like eating much.

"You've hardly touched your food," Ma says, examining your plate. "Is something wrong with it?"

"No, it's great," you say, picking at the cornmeal pudding with bits of bacon in it. "I'm just not feeling very hungry."

You see Ma exchange a worried look with Pa. You try to force yourself to take a few more bites, but the pudding won't go down your throat.

Later, as you lie in your tent, your legs ache and you have trouble falling asleep. Ma comes in to check on you while you are tossing and turning on your feather mat. You feel a cool hand on your forehead.

"You don't have a fever," Ma says. "I don't know what is wrong with you."

"I'll be okay, Ma," you say. "I probably just need to sleep."

But the next morning you feel even worse. You trudge along, even though it's hard to catch your breath. When everyone sits down to rest and snack during the midday break, you just rest your head on the side of the wagon. You can't eat anything at all.

Ma and Pa talk about what to do for you.

"I'm going to mix you up a drink of water, sugar,

and salt," Ma says. "That might help bring back some of your energy."

"Or what about a little citric acid mixed with some water and vinegar?" Pa suggests.

You don't feel like eating or drinking anything. But you know you have to take something. What do you ask for?

If you choose the sugar and salt drink, turn to page **46**

If you choose the citric acid mixture, turn to page **130**

Everyone agrees that the windlass sounds too risky to try. They want to stick to something more familiar, so they decide to just lead the oxen up the steep hill very slowly.

Pa tries to lighten the wagon for the animals by giving each of you something to carry. You have to haul a sack of coffee beans in a bag across your back.

The rocky hill proves tricky to climb. You watch each of your steps carefully to make sure you don't stumble. Pa leads the oxen up the hill, holding their yokes with a rope.

THUD!

One of the oxen slips on a rock and falls to his knees. The ox sharing his yoke falls, too. But with some coaxing, they get back on their feet and resume inching their way up the hill. When you finally get to the top, Pa takes a look at them and sadly shakes his head.

"I think this one might have a break in his leg," he says. "And the other one's knees look shaky."

"I'll clean them and wrap them up," Ma offers.

"That might help for now," Pa says. "But these animals will need time to heal. We can camp here for a few days and see if some rest is good enough. Or we can go back to Fort Bridger and see if they still have extra oxen for sale. That might save us some time."

What do you do?

If you head back to Fort Bridger, turn to page **51**

If you give the oxen some rest, turn to page **30**

If we try to run, the flames will just keep coming after us," Pa argues. "We won't be able to stop running."

You grab your bedrolls and some food from your wagon, and start leading the oxen up the mountains. Everyone is moving so quickly, it's hard not to stumble and slip on the rocks. You pull Hannah by the hand as you make your way upward. She tries her best to keep up, but at times you have to just yank her and drag her along.

"Faster!" Pa shouts.

As you climb, you feel the fire gaining on you. The air grows thick with smoke and it gets harder to breathe. You feel your legs start to burn with the exertion, and you cough from the smoke.

"Put this over your nose and mouth," Ma says, handing you a damp cloth. You try to breathe through it, and it helps. But as you scramble over a rock, the cloth falls from your hand.

You climb for what seems like forever. But it's working! You look behind you and see the forest ablaze, but you seem to be high enough that the flames won't reach you.

Pa finds a cave and you take shelter in it, huddled together, staring at each other in silence. Everyone is too exhausted and shocked to even speak. Your faces are covered with black soot and all you can make out is each other's eyes. If the situation weren't so scary, you would think it was funny.

Only one ox and your cow have survived the escape. Tears start to roll down your soot-covered face, dripping onto your lap. You are lucky to have survived, but you realize that the rest of your oxen and probably some people from your wagon train have perished in the fire. Your family decides to stay for a few days in the cave while Pa hunts for food. But then you'll have to figure out how to go on without your wagon or any supplies.

 **THE END**

No one is excited by the idea of going back to Fort Bridger. It was bad enough the first time around.

"I can't go back to that horrid place," Ma says.

"I still have nightmares about that rattler," Hannah adds.

Everyone agrees that the trip back isn't worth it, especially since you don't know what kind of animals they will have available for sale. Plus, everything you are forced to buy on the Trail is extremely expensive, so you might not even be able to afford a new set of oxen.

Instead, you make camp at the base of the Big Hill and wait for the animals to heal. The grazing conditions aren't great, but every day Pa scouts for the best place to let them eat and regain their strength.

After a few days, the oxen look better. Ma takes care of their dressing and thinks that the injuries are healing nicely. But the bad news is that while they improve, you are not feeling well at all. You start to have severe stomach pain and after a day or two you have diarrhea. By the time the oxen are ready to go, you are ready to move on, too . . . only not to Oregon Territory. You die of dysentery.

☞ **THE END**

teamboat Spring sounds more exciting to you, so you head there. Unlike other springs that hiss, this one spits out a stream of water, as tall as you, every fifteen seconds. The water whistles as it shoots up.

Being at the spring feels refreshing. One woman in your wagon train bakes bread with the soda water. It's the fluffiest bread you've had on the Trail. You camp and then trek four days to Fort Hall.

"Welcome," a tall man says as you arrive at the fort, a small stone building popular with fur traders and mountain men. The man, a fur trader named Henry, invites your group to supper. You're glad Ma and Pa accept, because you can smell something cooking that makes your mouth water.

A little while later, you sit at a table and poke at a pinkish steak on your plate. You wonder if it might still need to be cooked.

"What is this?" you whisper to Pa.

Henry just laughs.

"This is the finest of fish: Pacific salmon. Enjoy!"

You bite into the fish, which is unlike anything you've ever tasted. It's delicious! But then Henry says stuff that makes your stomach twist into knots.

"You know the most difficult part of the Trail is ahead of you—the mountains and the Columbia Valley. It's rough, with snow and dangerous rivers. I think it's crazy to take heavy wagons through it."

"Are you suggesting we stay here?" Pa asks.

"You could. But even better, you could go southwest, along the California Trail."

"Why that way?" Ma asks.

"It's easier, with greater rewards. Haven't you heard the stories of all the gold there?" Henry asks.

Pa is silent, but you can see that he is thinking about what Henry said. Ma looks worried and you know she is contemplating the dangers ahead.

Later, a few of the people in your wagon train start to talk about taking the California Trail. They don't want to deal with the harsh conditions on the Oregon Trail anymore, and they're tempted by the idea of gold.

Others want to continue to Oregon and fulfill their long-held dreams of free land promised to each family. They don't trust the fur trappers, who they think just want the territory to themselves. Others have made it, they argue. Why can't you?

It looks as if the train is going to split apart. What does your family decide to do?

If you take the California Trail, turn to page **122**

If you continue on the Oregon Trail, turn to page **139**

You pick at some of your food. Even though you're grateful for the gesture, you just can't bring yourself to eat any of it. While everyone else seems to enjoy the meal and conversation, you try to ignore the growling in your stomach.

"I noticed you didn't eat anything," Ma says as you walk back to camp. "You must be starving."

"I am," you admit, a little embarrassed.

"I'll make you some beans," Ma says, with an understanding look. "Fetch me some water from the wagon while I start a fire."

You hurry to the wagon, but in your haste, you accidentally grab the container of oily water that Pa uses to clean the wagon wheels when there is mud stuck on them. You hand it to Ma, who pours it into the pot and adds the beans.

You're so hungry you start eating right out of the pot, even though the beans haven't cooked all the way. They taste a little funny, but you eagerly eat them anyway.

Finally, with a full stomach, you go to bed. But you wake up in the middle of the night with stomach cramps. In the morning your cramps are much worse.

The next couple of days are terrible. You have chills and diarrhea. You even vomit! Ma and Pa are so concerned about you that they tell the wagon train to go ahead while they try to nurse you back to health. But soon they have to leave you behind. You die of dysentery.

☞ THE END

Let's go soak our feet first," you say, and Eliza leads the way. Archie runs along with you, barking excitedly. As you walk, a geyser suddenly erupts near you, and it startles everyone. You all laugh, but Archie takes off running in the other direction, scared.

"It's okay, boy, it's just water," you shout. But Archie continues to run farther away. You call for him a few times, but he doesn't listen to you.

"You guys stay and soak," you tell Joseph and Eliza. "I'm going to get Archie."

You run toward Archie and call him again. "Come on, boy, let's go." But now it's turned into a game. Archie wags his tail. He must want you to chase him.

"Here I come," you laugh, jumping over a few of the tiny springs that separate you. You are almost next to him, when one of the springs shoots off as you are jumping over it.

YOW! The water is scalding, and it feels like you are on fire. You fall to the ground in pain, screaming for help. Your arms and legs are severely burned.

Joseph comes rushing over to you. "What happened?" he says in a panic. And then his eyes grow wide as he sees your burns.

"Get help!" Joseph shouts to Eliza.

You lie there in a tremendous amount of pain. After a few moments you see that Ma, Pa, and Caleb are by your side. Your burns are so severe that they hesitate to move you. Ma gives you some cool water to drink and wraps you in the cleanest cloth she can find.

You won't be able to walk anytime soon. Even worse, you are at risk of terrible infection on the dirty Trail. You had no idea that some of the springs were hot enough to cook a steak. But as the water hisses and steams, your insides burn, and you realize that your dreams of getting to Oregon have just evaporated into thin air.

☞ **THE END**

Wait for me," you call out to Joseph, and run after him. You don't want him to snoop around by himself. And if he *does* find the animals, you want to be part of it. You imagine the looks on everyone's faces as you tell them where the missing animals are!

"Thanks for coming with me," Joseph says.

"What if we get caught?" you ask again, feeling your stomach flip over with nervousness.

"We can always say that we are lost," Joseph says. "No one is going to do anything to two kids."

Joseph speaks with confidence, so you try to push

your fear away and scramble to keep up with his long strides.

As you approach the wagon train, you hide behind a big rock so you can observe. There are a bunch of families going about their morning chores and making breakfast. Your stomach growls as you smell eggs frying. *Yum!* Your mouth starts to water.

"Look! They have chickens," you whisper to Joseph.

"Yeah," he mutters, counting their animals. "But it doesn't look like they have what we're looking for."

"What now?" you ask.

"Let's go to the Shoshone settlement."

"Okay," you say, although now you just want to go back to camp and have breakfast. You hope no one has noticed that you're missing yet. Ma gets worried really quickly.

As you approach the settlement, you can see Native American people, dressed in breechcloths and leggings, walking around. Several cooking fires are burning as the community prepares its own morning meal.

Joseph points to a tree. "Let's hide over there, and watch to see where they keep their animals," he says.

Your heart pounds as you get closer. Suddenly, a young boy spots you and starts to stare.

"Duck!" Joseph orders, pointing to a bush. You hide, but moments later a group of men, holding what look like spears, bows, and arrows, heads toward you.

"Look!" You grab on to Joseph's shirt. "What is happening?"

"It's okay," Joseph says. "Just let me do the talking."

"What are you going to say?" you ask, trying not to panic.

"I told you, I'll just tell them that we're lost," Joseph says.

"Let's just make a run for it," you say. "We can still get away."

You see Joseph deciding what to do. Do you stay still or start to run?

If you stay still, turn to page **77**

If you run back to camp, turn to page **18**

Let's look for higher ground," Ma encourages, while you and your siblings groan.

Pa nods. "I'm sorry we'll have to walk a bit more," he says, "but this way we won't have to worry about the river. It looks like it could flood."

You try to ignore the ache in your feet as you continue walking. Finally you find a spot which satisfies everyone, and at last you all stop.

Ma uses dried buffalo chips, dung that you've collected along the Trail, that she's saved for damp conditions to build your campfire. You help Pa make camp. It's too wet to set up tents, so you'll sleep in the wagon, as crowded as that is with all your stuff in it.

Once you sit down in front of the fire with a plate of hot food, everything seems better. But after you eat, you notice your throat is sore.

"Ma, my throat hurts," you say.

"Mine, too," Samuel adds.

Ma looks at you both and frowns.

"I'll make you some hot tea," she says. "And then you should get to bed early tonight."

The next morning, when you wake up, your throat is a little less sore. But you have a cough instead. Samuel is doing better and is running along the wagon as usual, kicking up dirt. The ground has dried out and the area you are walking through is dusty and bleak. There is nothing but sage bushes, and after a few miles of hiking, poor Archie is covered in what looks like ashes.

"I can hardly see anything but Archie's eyes," Hannah says, pointing at him. "Look!"

Your throat is tickling again so you take a swig from the water-skin and try not to cough from all the dust in the air. But at night, once you've settled on your soft feather bed, you start to cough a lot. After a while, you grow hoarse and your stomach hurts from all the coughing, but you still can't stop.

"Can you stop that, please?" Hannah complains. "I can't sleep! Can't you take some medicine?"

Samuel is snoring, but Hannah is a light sleeper. You try to stifle your coughs, but it doesn't help.

Caleb keeps a medicine chest, including tonics, that help with coughs. Maybe you should take some. Caleb always says yes when anyone asks for medicine, but you don't want to wake him. Maybe you should just go get the medicine yourself. What do you do?

If you take some of the tonic, turn to page **113**

If you just try to sleep without it, turn to page **117**

You slowly sip on water that is mixed with generous amounts of salt and sugar. Even though it makes you gag, it helps you to feel a little stronger. But over the next few days, the pain in your legs gets worse. Your legs tingle and throb all day long and keep you awake at night. Eventually you are so wobbly, it feels like you've forgotten how to walk. Pa spreads out your feather bed and lays you down in the wagon. The bumpy ride mixed with the smell of the oxen makes you feel nauseous, and you have to keep a bucket next to you.

As the days go by you start to feel more and more terrible. Then your gums start to bleed and the next day you are horrified to find your teeth have actually become loose. Only they're not your baby teeth. As you get sicker and sicker, everyone else in your family starts to feel ill, too. Hannah and Samuel cry because their legs hurt, and because they are scared to end up looking and feeling like you. They're right to be scared, because you will eventually die of scurvy.

☞ THE END

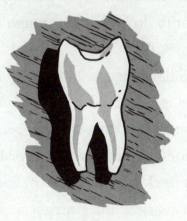

We'll just make camp here," Ma tells you, much to your relief. It's been a long day of hiking and the last thing you want to do is traipse through more mud to find another spot.

Ma tries to light the few buffalo chips she's saved for an emergency, but it's too damp to get a fire started. So instead you eat a cold supper of buffalo jerky and prairie biscuits, then go to bed. Even though there's food in your stomach, you're not fully satisfied. You fall asleep imagining a sizzling steak with mashed potatoes and green beans, complete with a nice slice of chocolate cake for dessert.

BOOM! CRASH!

"What's that?" Hannah's wide eyes peer at you from under her blanket. You've all been startled awake by a violent thunderstorm.

"It's just thunder," you say, trying to sound brave. Archie whimpers and nestles his body against yours. "Everything will be okay. Try to go back to sleep."

But it's impossible for any of you to fall asleep as long as the storm lasts. Each time the thunder claps, you jump, and the sound of the wind howling is worse than coyotes. The rain pours down with such force that it bends the tent. Finally, after what seems like hours, the rain starts to slow down. You drift back to sleep.

You wake to a different scary sound: shouting, from outside your tent. You poke your head outside and gaze in horror at what you see. Half the camp seems to have vanished, including heavy stuff like boxes of dishes and the animals' yokes. Some of the wagons are filled with water, their contents floating under the canopies.

"What happened?" you ask Ma. "Is this just from the thunderstorm?"

"It looks like flash floods," she replies grimly. "It was a mistake to camp here. We should have known that the water level was too high, and the ground was too wet."

"The storm just did us in," Pa adds, shaking his head. "It would have been safer to keep moving to higher ground to camp."

Your family didn't lose as much as everyone else, but you've lost enough to keep you from going farther. Entire sacks of flour have been torn open and filled with water. Without your food supply, the risks of starving on the Trail are too great to continue. In a flash, your dreams of Oregon are over.

☞ **THE END**

You are going to try to make it back to Fort Bridger to get more oxen. Pa suggests that Ma stay camped with Hannah and Samuel at Big Hill while the two of you hike to Fort Bridger. It's nice to have some time alone with Pa. Along the way, he tells you stories of his childhood in Kentucky.

When you arrive at Fort Bridger, traders approach you with an offer to sell you oxen.

"That's four times what I paid back in Missouri!" Pa cries. "I don't have that kind of money."

"I'll tell you what," one man says. "I can give you these two mules for the price of one ox."

Pa looks unsatisfied but knows he doesn't have many options. He hands over the money and you head back to Big Hill. The mules are a little difficult to guide along the way, but Pa thinks they just have to get used to their new owners. He suggests tying the animals to a tree and making camp. You loosen the ropes that have been holding the mule you've been leading.

OW!

Once it's free, the mule kicks you in the stomach and runs off, back toward Fort Bridger. You fall to the ground, clutching your gut. Pa gets kicked, too, except in the leg.

"I think it's broken!" Pa says, unable to stand.

You help Pa as he limps back to the rest of your family. Unfortunately, you'll have to return to Fort Bridger while Pa gets medical help. You hate the fort and the idea of being there any longer, but for now it's where your dreams end. Be sure to keep an eye out for snakes!

 **THE END**

You decide to head to the lake by yourself, planning to surprise everyone with the filled water-skins. Then in the morning, you can take everyone back to see the lake for themselves and refill your water barrels for the rest of the journey through the desert. You imagine Ma's face lit up with her biggest smile, the one that means she is bursting with happiness. And you wonder if maybe Caleb will agree to let everyone go for a quick swim before you have to head back on the hot dusty Trail. You always feel so dirty on the road, and on this stretch you've felt extra sweaty and grimy.

As you walk toward the lake, you can't wait to dip your hands into the crystal clear water and wash them clean. Then you'll drink the cool water to your heart's content. You know it will be the most refreshing and delicious water you've ever tasted.

You walk a little faster, admiring how the rays of the sun are reflecting on the water. The water sparkles and shimmers and is the deepest color of turquoise. But it's still so far away. As you stumble over a rock,

you notice that you don't seem to be getting any closer, even though you've been walking for a long time now. The lake must be farther away than it seemed. You decide that it must be hard to estimate distance with nothing but sand around you.

You start to run toward the lake. You're panting heavily and your legs are tired, but you can't stop now. But no matter how hard you run, the lake only seems to get farther away. Your head is hurting now, and you start to feel dizzy. For a moment it looks as if there are two lakes instead of one. You stop and blink hard.

You wonder why you're feeling so strange. *What's happening to me?*

Soon your legs buckle and you fall to the ground. You can't move another muscle and your head is pounding. You have severe heat exhaustion. The lake is only a mirage. You think you see something that's not really there. But what *is* real is the fact that you've been wandering in the hot desert for a while and no one knows where you are. Your chances of being found are extremely low.

☞ **THE END**

The snake is looking you straight in the face. Its head keeps swaying from side to side as its pointy tongue flickers. It feels like you have been lying there for hours, but only a few moments have passed. You try to move your arm slowly to the side, but you see the snake's head follow your motion, as if it can anticipate your next move.

You're so terrified that you just can't take it anymore. You jump up from the floor. "Snake!" you scream at the top of your lungs.

Before you get very far, you feel an intense pain as fangs pierce the skin on your leg. As quickly as the snake has struck you, it slithers away. You fall to the ground. Everyone else wakes up from your howling.

"What happened?" Pa asks.

A warm tingle travels through your body. You can barely speak.

"S-s-s-nakebite," you finally say, and point to your leg.

"What kind? Where did it go?" Pa says, with panic in his voice.

"It was a rattler," you manage to whisper.

Your eyes start to roll back in your head, and the last thing you see is Pa's stricken face as he cradles you in his arms.

☞ **THE END**

Getting off the Trail is too scary to consider, you decide. Who knows what you might find? It's safer to stick to the road others have traveled before you.

You continue along the path, but before it gets any better, it gets worse. The conditions become harsher. You enter into an area that is nothing but desert.

"I'm so hot," Samuel complains. He takes off his hat and mops his face, which is red and sunburnt.

You don't even have the energy to reply, so you just concentrate on moving one foot in front of the next. Your legs feel like lead and all you want to do is sit down with a cold glass of lemonade.

"I'm thirsty," Hannah whines.

Ma and Pa are saving most of the water you have left for the family. The oxen are struggling to keep moving, and you're afraid that they will eventually collapse and die. You've seen piles of animal bones along the Trail, bleached by the hot sun.

As it gets harder to keep moving, your wagon train starts to travel by night instead of day, to avoid the intense sun. It feels weird and a bit spooky to move in the dark, led by the light of a couple of lanterns, and you are forced to move slowly to avoid stumbling. But your oxen team continues to get weaker. The animals are moving slower and slower every day.

After a night's hike, everyone is too hot and tired to even consider building a fire. You eat a cold supper of jerky, cold beans, and cornbread. And your family talks about what to do moving forward.

"I'm afraid that we can't continue like this without the oxen dying on us," Pa says. "If we don't get them some grass or water soon, we'll be stranded."

"But we don't know when we'll find those things," Ma points out.

"That's true," Pa continues. "So that leaves us with a hard choice."

A feeling of dread settles over you.

"We can unload as much as possible from our wagons to make the load lighter for the oxen,"

Pa says. "That means dumping everything that isn't essential."

"What's the other option?" Ma asks.

"We can abandon the wagon and carry as much as we can on our backs. A wagon might not be able to cross the mountains that are up ahead anyway. This way, we load up the oxen with some supplies, but it will be easier for them than pulling the wagon."

Everyone in your family falls quiet as you think about what makes the most sense. What do you decide?

If you unload your wagon, turn to page 95

If you abandon the wagon, turn to page 90

You decide that traveling by night will be too dangerous, since it will be hard to see where you are going. Plus you would hate to run into bandits or coyotes roaming the desert. Instead, you form a wide line, leaving plenty of space between each wagon, and start to move forward that way. It helps some, and you find that you cough less with fewer dust clouds in the air.

But even with this adjustment, you're still drinking too much of the water you've brought. At this pace, you will run out really soon. Everyone starts to cut down on the amount of water the animals get, to save more for the people, but that just makes the oxen weaker. You see them struggling.

"We need to find a water source, quickly," Caleb says, "before the animals start to die."

"But we can't! That will mean going off the Trail," Ma protests.

"And we don't know where or when we will find anything," another man says. "We could just end up wandering around longer in the desert heat."

"What if we send out a search party for water while the rest of the group rests and stays camped?" someone suggests.

"That could be dangerous," Pa says. "We should stick together."

"We have to do something," Caleb says. "What will it be?"

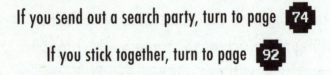

If you send out a search party, turn to page **74**

If you stick together, turn to page **92**

You reluctantly break off a little piece of the root cake and nibble on it. Not bad! Pa was right. It does taste a lot like a sweet potato. You hungrily eat a big piece.

"How is the stew?" you ask Joseph. He is licking his fingers, satisfied.

"It's really good," he says with a big grin.

You take a small bite and realize he's right. In the end, you have a pretty tasty meal, although you stay away from the bear root bread.

After everyone has eaten, your hosts serve you some berries and nuts for dessert along with a fragrant hot tea. Then a young man, wearing beaded moccasins and leather pants with fringe on the sides, gets up and everyone hushes.

A moment later, someone starts to bang on a drum while others chant and the man starts to dance in a way that you have never seen. His body bends and he stomps gracefully in a pattern, making circles on the ground. His hair is long and sleek and he is holding a feathered bow. It looks like he is using his body to tell a story of hunting, and the drumming and chanting gets louder and softer as he moves faster and slower.

When the dancer is done, another gets up and tells a different story. You can't take your eyes off of the performers, each one more graceful than the last. Everyone else is completely fascinated, too. And so the night continues until Samuel starts to nod off and Ma motions that it is time to head back to camp.

⭐ ⭐ ⭐

The next morning, it's time to part with Roaring Cloud, Bright Sky, and the rest of the people you have met. You feel a lump in your throat as Roaring Cloud looks you in the eye and nods slowly.

"Goodbye," you say, wondering if you'll ever see him again. Hannah runs to give him a hug. Roaring Cloud looks surprised at first, but then you see him hold her tight for a few seconds.

You spend the day traveling to Fort Bridger. Everyone is looking forward to getting there in order to replenish much-needed supplies and make repairs to their wagons. Plus, it's been awhile since you were at a place with buildings and traders. But when you arrive at the well-known Fort Bridger, it's not what you expect at all.

"That's it?" Eliza grumbles. "Those hardly look like log cabins!"

You can't believe your eyes, either. Fort Bridger is a collection of a few rickety wooden buildings belonging to the fur trappers who live here with their

Native American wives. They don't have much to trade—mostly furs, skins, moccasins, and blankets.

Ma is the most disappointed of all; she was hoping to send letters back home and buy some more molasses. But at least there is a blacksmith shop, where Pa gladly gets shoes for the oxen and replaces your cow.

That night, when you're sleeping in one of the wooden huts instead of your tent, Archie curls up by your feet as usual. But then, suddenly, he growls.

"Shush, Archie," you say, and start to roll over. But then you freeze. On your feather mat, staring right at you, is a big rattlesnake! You hear the rattling sound, and it makes your heart stop. Do you jump up and run away from the snake as fast as you can, or lie still and hope that it leaves you alone?

If you run away, turn to page **56**

If you lie still, turn to page **143**

You're too afraid of the quick-moving current to let go of the rope you're holding on to, even though you're a good swimmer. Instead, you scream as loudly as you can. "Somebody, grab that wheel!"

You see a man from your wagon train try to reach for it, but he misses. Joseph then attempts to catch the wheel with a rope, but he isn't successful, either. The wheel continues to float down the river, and your heart sinks as you watch it disappear out of sight.

"Pa!" you shout again, breathlessly. "We lost our wagon wheel!"

Pa turns around to see what is happening. As he checks to make sure everything else in the wagon is secure, one of your oxen loses his footing on the soft sand of the river bottom. The ox stumbles and falls over, pulling down the animal attached to him. Soon the two oxen are tangled in their yokes, and are suddenly swept underwater.

"Get up!" Pa yells, as he desperately tries to pull them up onto their feet. But they are just too big and difficult to handle. You try to help, but the oxen are thrashing so wildly you're afraid one kick from their powerful legs will knock you out.

Finally Pa gives up. "We have to keep moving," he shouts, with a grim expression. Slowly you make it to the first island.

Your family assesses the damages. The two oxen have drowned, and your wheel is gone. You may be able to get to the other side of the river, but after that, your wagon isn't going anywhere. Many other families in the wagon train have also lost animals, items from their wagons, and in one case, an entire wagon that flipped over.

Everyone huddles on the island, afraid to cross the next part of the river and dreading what's ahead. Even if you make it back to solid land, you'll have to make some hard choices about what to do next. Getting to Oregon City seems impossible now.

 **THE END**

You walk over to where your father is talking to a group of men.

"Excuse me, Pa?" you say, hesitant to interrupt.

"What is it?" Pa asks.

"I have something to tell you," you continue, motioning that you want him to step aside with you.

Pa walks away from the Shoshone to listen to you privately. You tell him about Joseph's plan to spy on the other camp and the Indian settlement to look for the missing animals. He looks at you with concern.

"That is a terrible idea!" he says. "He could get lost, or be accused of stealing himself. It's a good thing you told me."

Pa rushes over to Caleb and tells him what happened. They team up with another two men and head out to track down Joseph.

"Where did he go first?" Caleb asks.

"To the other camp we passed, I think," you say, not wanting to meet Caleb's eye. What if he blames you for letting Joseph go?

You wait anxiously with Ma, pacing until everyone returns. Finally, after what seems like hours, you see them walking back. *Phew!* Joseph is with them and you breathe a big sigh of relief.

Joseph walks right by without even looking at you. You know he's really upset. But Pa tells you that the other wagon train didn't have your animals, and they were actually in really bad shape themselves.

"They said they had been through enough and were ready to go back," he explains. "They weren't interested in anything other than the fastest route home."

"Then what about the stolen animals?" Ma asks.

"We just have to forget about them," Pa says. "Anyone could have taken them. We may never find them and we don't have time to waste trying to track them down."

"We'll just have to be extra careful from now on,"

Caleb adds. He pats you on the shoulder, giving you a look that means that everything will be okay.

Over the next couple days, every time you try to talk to Joseph, he turns away and ignores you. But finally, he starts to speak to you again.

"I guess it was a bad idea for me to go off like that," he says. "And you were only looking out for me." You just nod, and the matter is over. You're back to being friends. It's too lonely on the Trail to let small arguments ruin a friendship.

The next day, you arrive at the infamous Green River Crossing. The river is known to be difficult to cross, especially in the spring, when the winter snows melt and raise the water levels, creating strong currents. This time of year, in July, the water is a little lower, but you still have to walk across the river on narrow gravel bars. Another option is to use the ferry that some mountain men have created, but they charge a fee.

When you arrive at the crossing, the area around it has been transformed into a big camping site. You see lots of other travelers, and rut marks of other wagons that have come before you. As you make camp, Caleb goes to find out how much the ferry will cost you.

A bit later he returns, slowly shaking his head with disappointment.

"The ferry is being repaired," he says. "It will take at least four days to get it running again."

Four days! That is a long time to wait and it will delay you. There is a line of wagons already ahead of you. At the same time, the ferry might be the safer option, even if it is the more expensive one. Everyone debates the two choices: crossing the river yourselves or waiting for the ferry. What do you decide?

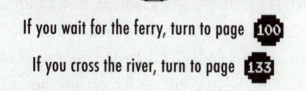

If you wait for the ferry, turn to page **100**

If you cross the river, turn to page **133**

Caleb organizes a small group of men to leave with him to search for water.

"How much water do you have left?" Caleb asks.

"If we ration what we have, we should be okay for about three days," Pa replies.

As the search party leaves, everyone is silent.

"I think it's a mistake for us to split up," Ma says firmly.

"I agree, but I hope they come back with water soon," Pa replies.

Everyone's patience is running low from being thirsty and overheated, so you organize a game for Samuel, Hannah, Eliza, and Joseph. You climb under your wagon where it's shady and take turns making shadow puppets and guessing what the shapes are. For a few moments everyone forgets how hot it is.

After two more days, you are running drastically low on water. Pa says that if the search party does not return soon you will have to move ahead without them and look for water yourselves. You look at

Eliza's and Joseph's sad faces and imagine how worried they must be about their father.

The next day, when there is still no sign of the search party, Pa says you must leave.

"Don't worry about Caleb," he says to Eliza and Joseph to reassure them. "I'm sure he will find us."

You get back on the Trail, but within a few hours one of your oxen collapses. One by one, each wagon starts to lose animals.

Two more of your oxen lie down, and you tug on their yoke to encourage them to get back up. You feel a warm wind kicking up behind you, sending little pieces of sand flying and getting in your eyes. Within minutes you are caught in the midst of a fierce sandstorm. The powerful wind and swirling hot sand pelt you relentlessly. There's no place to hide, and even though you cover your nose and mouth with your shirt, sand still gets through. You fall to your knees, try to protect your face, and wait for the storm to pass.

When the sandstorm dies down, you cough up bits of sand and begin to search for your family. You discover Hannah crying because another pair of oxen have died. Your family is stranded without any water, any animals to pull your wagon, and, soon, any hopes of survival.

☞ THE END

Help!" Joseph says, coming out of the bush with his hands raised.

You stand behind him as the Native men approach you.

"We lost a cow and a horse," Joseph continues. "Can you help us?"

"We haven't seen your animals," says the youngest of the men.

"Someone stole them last night," you say.

The young man speaks to an older man wearing a rabbit fur robe. Then he turns back to you.

"There is a tribe known for stealing animals. What they do is wrong. We will get your animals back," the man says. "Where is your wagon train?"

Joseph tells them and looks at you with a big smile. You head back to camp, excited to tell the others the good news.

"Where have you been?" Pa says, furious, when he sees you. "We've been looking everywhere for you!"

"But Pa," you start to say.

"I can't believe you would disappear like that, without telling anyone where you went," Pa continues. "Your mother is worried sick."

You feel terrible, and hope that Joseph is having a better time breaking the news to his dad. But later Joseph comes around looking glum.

"Pa didn't want to hear anything about what we found out," he says. "He was so angry!"

But a little while later you see the Shoshone people you encountered earlier walking up to your camp. And they have your missing animals!

Your wagon train welcomes them and invites them to a feast. Everyone cooks up the best meal possible, with one wagon member breaking out tins of fruit saved from the beginning of your travels on the Trail. And you send the people of the Shoshone Nation back to their settlement laden with gifts.

That gives Pa a big idea.

"I'm sorry I got so upset at you," he says. "I think your meeting these people is one of the best things that has happened to us in a while."

Pa explains that he wants to start a business with the local people, offering services to other pioneers. "We can help people who have lost animals, want guides, or need food and water," Pa says. "And I'm sure people will want to trade and buy things from us, which will make us a good living!"

Your family's dreams of getting to Oregon aren't gone forever, just on hold for a little while.

☞ **THE END**

Eliza," you call out softly, tapping her on the shoulder as she sleeps in the shade of her wagon.

"What time is it?" she asks, still groggy. "Do we have to start walking again already?"

"Not yet. It's still the afternoon," you say. "But I have to show you something incredible."

Eliza sits up now, looking curious. "What is it?"

"I found a lake!" you say. "Will you go with me to get some water? We can surprise everyone when they wake up."

Eliza gives you a puzzled look.

"A lake?" she asks. "That's impossible. We're in the middle of a desert."

"No, look! It's right over there." You point toward the shimmering water.

Eliza looks at you with concern now. She tells you that you're just seeing a mirage, which is something that isn't really there, and gives you a few sips of water to drink. Then she wakes up Ma and Pa.

Ma touches your skin gently. "You're burning up!" she says.

You start to feel a little nauseous and lie down, and soon you pass out. You have heat stroke and are breathing rapidly. Everyone is trying to get your body temperature down any way they can. But there isn't much they can do without cold water or ice.

Luckily you *do* wake up, but you are much too weak to continue on this journey. And pretty soon, without any water, the rest of your family is feeling the same as you. You never imagined that something as simple—but as precious—as water would end up destroying your dreams of Oregon.

☞ **THE END**

It's decided," Caleb says, after everyone agrees. "We'll float the wagons across the river."

A couple days later, you reach the infamous crossing of the Snake River. You make camp early along the banks of the river, and spend the rest of the day preparing for what's ahead. Next comes the big task of unloading the wagons and taking them apart. Everyone helps. Once your wagon is empty, Pa gets to work removing the axles and the wheels. That leaves him with the box of the wagon, which he caulks and seals carefully with wax to make it as waterproof as possible.

Caleb suggests keeping the animals yoked, so they'll be easier to lead through the water, even though they won't be pulling the wagons. When

everything is ready, you walk to the banks of the river and gaze out over the wide expanse you'll have to cross. The water rushes by swiftly, and the current is a little frightening. It makes you gulp.

"We'll hold on tight to the animals or to the wagon as we cross," Ma says, seeing your face. "It'll be okay."

Ma isn't as strong a swimmer as you, so you know she must be nervous. You smile and nod as reassuringly as you can. But inside, you're still a little scared, too.

The next morning, you form a line and make your way into the water. You're heading for the first island. The cold water comes up to your waist and you grab on tight to the ropes, leading the oxen, feeling safer as the oxen move slowly but steadily through the water.

"Hold 'em steady," Pa says, looking behind him to make sure everyone is following.

You look behind you, too, and suddenly you see one of your wagon wheels slip out of the wagon. It starts to float away! It will get swept into the current and disappear downstream. But you could still reach it—it's only a few feet away from you.

You pause for a second, deciding whether you should swim after it and grab it. Wagon wheels are difficult to replace on the Trail, and you don't have any more spares. Or you could just stay where you are and hope that someone else grabs it. What do you do?

If you swim after the wagon wheel, turn to page **98**

If you stay where you are, turn to page **67**

After a vote, it is decided that you're going to build the windlass. This way you have less chance of injuring the animals or damaging your wagons on the steep climb. Even though it will take some time and effort, everyone decides that it's worth trying.

Caleb volunteers his wagon to be used for the windlass. The first step is to empty it out and push it up the hill. Then Pa puts his carpentry skills to work, using ropes and wheels to make a pulley at the

top of the hill. Soon you have an impressive device connected to trees at the bottom of the hill.

You watch nervously as the first wagon makes the trip up Big Hill. It works! The animals are led up slowly next, taking lots of breaks along the way. And finally, after several hours, all of the wagons safely make it up the hill. Joseph is so proud that his idea worked. And you're impressed by Pa's handy skills.

Everyone takes a break at the top of the hill, eating leftover breakfast as a midday snack. Next comes the tricky task of making it down the steep slope. You remember how difficult it was to get down a sharp incline at Alcove Spring, back in the second week of your journey. You used ropes to tie your wagon wheels and make brakes, and it took the strength of all the men to slowly bring the wagons down the hill. This hill is even steeper.

Since it would be so easy to lose control of the wagons, you take all of the same precautions. Then the men hold on to the wagons with ropes and lead them down the hill in a zigzag pattern instead of straight down. A few items fall out of the wagons, but you manage to get down safely.

The rest of the hills you have to surmount are nothing compared to Big Hill, so it's smooth going for the next few days.

One afternoon, Samuel runs up to you. "Guess what's coming up next?" he asks.

"What?" you reply, hoping it's something good.

"Soda Springs!" he says, a note of wonder in his voice. "Pa says the water tastes like it comes from a real soda fountain." You can't remember the last time you drank soda water, but it sure sounds refreshing right now.

"Ma says we can add sugar to the fizzy water for a special treat," Hannah adds with a big smile.

You know right away when you've reached Soda Springs. Everyone marvels at the bizarre landscape, which is unlike anything you've ever seen before. You stare at cone-shaped geysers as tall as Pa, spewing water like miniature volcanoes. There are craters of all sizes and waterfalls, too. But most fascinating of all are the springs, some of which make gurgling and hissing sounds and have steam rising above them.

After everyone finds a spot to camp, you all grab your cups and follow Caleb to one of the soda springs. He is the first to dip his cup in and take a big sip.

"It smells a little funny, but it sure tastes great," he says, grinning.

As promised, Ma has allowed you to add some sugar to your cup. You carefully taste the sweet fizzy water, enjoying the way it tickles your tongue. You're amazed that it came right out of the ground like that!

After you drink your fill, Ma and Pa say that you can explore this wondrous area a little bit with Eliza and Joseph.

"Just be careful," Ma says.

"Let's go," Joseph says. "Can you hear that?"

You hear a high-pitched whistle that reminds you of the steamboats you saw in Missouri.

Joseph points in the direction the sound is coming from. "That's coming from a place called Steamboat Spring. Let's go there!"

"Wait!" Eliza says, "I'd rather go to the hot springs and soak my feet."

Both options sound fun to you. Which do you agree to do?

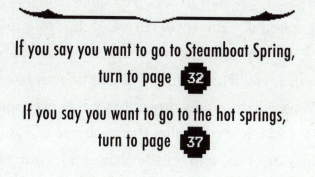

If you say you want to go to Steamboat Spring,
turn to page **32**

If you say you want to go to the hot springs,
turn to page **37**

Pa decides that the smartest thing to do is to abandon the wagon and continue on foot. You see the fear on your family's faces at the thought, but Pa explains that it is your best chance of survival.

You've had a long night of hiking, so Pa suggests you get as much sleep as possible.

"Everyone will have to carry supplies from here on," he says.

As your eyes start to shut, you can see the sun rising in the sky. You try to fall asleep, but your mind is racing with the image of the white, sun-bleached bones of animals you have passed. Will that be your fate, too?

When the sun goes down, Ma wakes everyone up. Pa has laid out the supplies that each one of you will be carrying. You strap on your bag and set out, trying to ignore the weight on your shoulders. You overhear Ma and Pa talking.

"How much food and water do you think we have?" Ma asks.

"If we are careful, we can probably make it for

five days, but after that we have to find some water," Pa responds.

★ ★ ★

You have been walking for four days now.

"I think we should stop walking for tonight," Pa eventually says.

You drop your bag to the ground, and you see Samuel reach for the water-skin.

"Let me have some when you're done," you say.

He takes a small sip, walks over to you, and hands you the pouch. You put it to your mouth and just a few drops come out. It's the same with the rest of the water-skins. They are all empty.

You search desperately for water. But there is nothing. Your family cannot survive. As you lie down for the night, parched and weak, you wonder who will pass by *your* bones.

 **THE END**

I'm so glad that we stuck together," Ma says.

"The idea of splitting up didn't sit well with me, either," Pa responds.

Caleb holds a quick meeting about the water shortage situation.

"We have to be extra careful from here on out," he says. "We are dangerously low on water and I don't want anyone to get dehydrated."

You know that Pa has been drinking the least amount of water in your family. He has been trying to make sure that Samuel and Hannah have more. Your brother and sister each passed out once already in the last few days, and Ma keeps staring at their faces to make sure they are not overheating again.

"Pa, do you see that?" You point into the distance, where some riders are on horseback. The dust the horses are kicking up creates a cloud.

Soon they have caught up to your wagon.

"How are you doing today?" one of the men asks.

"It sure is hot out here," another adds.

"Which way you folks headed?" a third man chimes in.

Caleb exchanges glances with Pa and a few others in the wagon train.

"We have some water if you folks are interested," the last man says.

Samuel is quick to respond. "We sure do need some water, mister," he says.

The man reaches into a pouch on the horse and pulls out a container of water.

"It's going to be fifteen dollars a cup," he says.

"That's robbery!" Pa exclaims.

Pa and the men begin arguing and you start to get scared when the strangers shout angrily, right before they ride away. One of them reaches into his back pocket, pulls out a gun, and shoots.

BANG! BANG!

You can hear the gunshots ringing in your ears for some time. And then when they stop, you see that a bullet has ricocheted off of a large rock and hit Caleb in the leg! Luckily the bullet went through his leg cleanly, but it will still take several weeks for your wagon captain to heal.

While you're waiting, Pa discovers a freshwater spring with clear and delicious water. As you camp there, Ma and Pa start to sell fresh pies, quilts, and other goods to thirsty travelers who stop to rest. By the time Caleb is ready to move on, your family is settled, happy, and convinced that this is a better life than the one on the Trail. You watch the rest of the wagon train roll away, as you help yourself to a big piece of pie.

☞ **THE END**

You decide to unload the wagon as much as possible to make it easier on the oxen. But that means that you are down to the bare essentials for the rest of your journey. You are sad to see the pile of stuff that you are forced to leave behind, from most of your dishes and your only pair of nice clothes, to all of the supplies Pa brought with you for the farm. All you're left with is your bedrolls, camping supplies, work clothes, and most important of all, food.

The idea works. Your oxen team manages to pull the lighter wagon out of the desert and into the Sierra Nevada mountain range. It's beautiful and scenic and a welcome change, even if the Trail takes you over a rocky and at times steep path. It's nice to see trees, and making camp is easier with plenty of wood for the fire.

Things are going well until one day you see a pair of rabbits dash toward you and keep running past

your wagon train. Before you can tell anyone, several mule deer appear from the woods, running at full speed in the same direction as the rabbits.

"Look, Pa!" you shout, pointing to the backs of the deer as they disappear out of sight. "Where are these animals running to?"

As you speak, some big-horned sheep come tearing out of the trees. Birds flee into the air.

"I think the bigger question is, What are these animals running *away from?*" Pa says.

Ma points above the trees. "There's smoke over there!" You look to the right and see a low cloud of dark smoke.

"It must be a forest fire!" Pa says, with urgency in his voice. "We have to get out of here before it reaches us."

You feel fear gripping your heart. "What should we do?" you ask.

"Let's run!" Ma says. "Leave everything behind and follow those animals!"

"Wait," Pa says. "We could try to outrun the fire.

But we could also try to climb high enough into the mountains to be out of harm's way."

"What about the animals?" Ma asks.

"We can try to take them with us," Pa says.

"What about our things?" you ask.

"Just grab what you can carry easily," Ma says. "Whether we run or climb, we can't take too much."

You don't have long to decide what to do. The smoke is heading your way, and you can smell burning now. What do you choose?

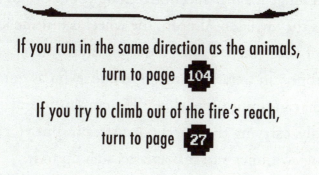

If you run in the same direction as the animals, turn to page 104

If you try to climb out of the fire's reach, turn to page 27

You lunge for the wheel, stretching your arms out as far as they will go. Almost! The wheel is just inches out of your reach. Taking a deep breath, you let go of the rope you were holding on to and swim as quickly as you can toward the wheel. The current is moving rapidly, carrying the wheel downstream. But you are a strong swimmer and manage to catch up to it.

Got it! You wrap your fingers around the wheel, and pull it close to you. It's still floating and starts to carry you like a raft.

"Pa!" you shout, realizing that no one saw you swim away and that they won't know where you are.

You see Pa moving the oxen along, and try to wave to get his attention. But your family and wagon are only getting smaller as you move farther and farther away.

Desperate, you use all your strength to swim in their direction. Your muscles start to burn, but you can't make any progress against the powerful current. It continues to pull you away from where you want to be. Suddenly, you see some rocks in front of you. You manage to steer the wheel and yourself away from them just in time.

BAM! The next rocks are too big to avoid. You crash into them, and right before you are knocked out forever, you wonder if the wagon wheel will still make it to shore.

☞ **THE END**

Almost everyone agrees to wait for the ferry to be repaired. Even though it will take a few days, you've heard too many stories of pioneers slipping and falling off the gravel path into the swift current of the Green River. Many wagons were lost this way, and both dreams and lives were destroyed.

Luckily the banks of the Green River make for a nice, grassy place to camp where the animals can graze. Pa and Caleb volunteer to help repair the ferry, which gets it operating a day sooner.

When it's finally your time to ride across, you sit in the wagon, which is taken over the rushing water on a wooden planked raft. You hold your little brother's and sister's hands tightly until you are safely across to the other side.

It takes almost a full day for all of the wagons in your train to get across the river. While you're waiting, you, Joseph, and Eliza organize the kids into a game of hide-and-seek.

"You're it!" Samuel shouts and runs away.

You close your eyes and count to fifty.

"Ready or not, here I come," you announce, and look around. No one is in sight except for Archie, who barks and runs toward a bunch of bushes. You follow him to see what he finds.

When you get to the bushes, you hear Archie start to growl softly.

"It's okay, Archie," you say, expecting to see your little brother or sister curled up there. But instead, you gasp. Lying in the brush next to a little pond is a baby antelope! It stares at you with wide round eyes.

"Aw, poor thing," you say. "Why are you all alone?"

You guess the antelope has been orphaned or abandoned, so you go ask Ma if you can give it a little bit of milk in a cup.

"You shouldn't touch wild animals!" she says, following you to the spot. But when she sees the baby animal, she softens and agrees to give you some milk.

The antelope follows you and becomes your new pet. You name her Gertrude and tie a ribbon around her neck. When the wagon train moves, she travels with you, just like Archie.

One afternoon, after you've stopped for your midday break, a bunch of dogs appear out of nowhere and start chasing Gertrude. A moment later, two Lakota men on horses race after the dogs. You run after them, waving your arms and yelling.

"Stop! She's mine!"

A little while later, the Lakota men return with Gertrude tied to the back of a horse, lying limp.

"No!" you cry, realizing the dogs must have caught up to her.

One of the men gets off his horse and speaks to Pa. After the conversation, Pa approaches you.

"The men are sorry their dogs killed your antelope," he says. "They are offering us some deerskins in return."

It's nice of the Lakota people to want to give you something in return for what happened to Gertrude.

But part of you feels like you shouldn't accept it. Their dogs didn't know Gertrude was your pet. What do you say?

If you say that you'll take the gift, turn to page **21**

If you decline the gift, turn to page **108**

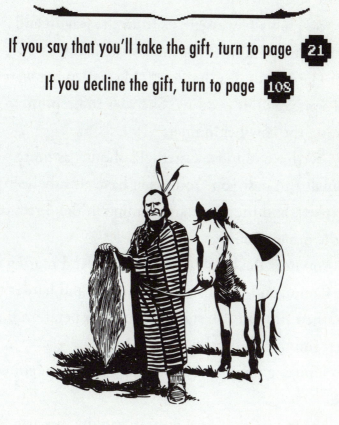

Let's run," Ma says. "I'm afraid we won't be able to climb quickly enough, and the animals won't make it up the steep incline."

You grab a few essentials from the wagon and start to run. You hold Samuel by the hand, and Pa puts Hannah on his shoulders. Ma is carrying water and some of your bedding. She tries to keep up, leading the cow behind her.

"We have to move faster!" Pa shouts, as more wild animals run past you. Your oxen have already been unyoked, and they, too, are running in the direction of the other animals.

You hear the breaking of branches and roaring of the flames, and the smoke gets thicker and harder to breathe through. You start to cough desperately, but keep running as quickly as you can.

"You're going too fast," Samuel says. "I'm going to fall!"

"Keep up," you snap at him, yanking his arm. You feel bad for being harsh, but you know there is no other option. Sam has to keep running, even though his legs must be aching as badly as yours.

You feel the heat of the fire grow more intense. It gets harder and harder to keep moving, and more and more difficult to breathe.

"Sam!" you shout as your little brother stumbles and falls to the ground. He lies there, unmoving.

"Sam! Get up!" You shake him hard and roll him over, and see a big gash on his head.

Pa runs back and grabs Sam, handing Hannah off to Ma. You start to run again and for a moment everything seems quiet. You think you might have gotten away from the fire, and wonder if maybe it turned in a different direction. But you're wrong. Within moments the fire catches up to all of you and you are engulfed in flames.

☞ **THE END**

The group decides the cutoff is the better way to go. Not only will you save a week of travel, you won't have to ford the Green River. Everyone tries to prepare for the challenges of the desert ahead. Your water-skins are fully loaded, and you've brought along extra barrels of water.

"It's important to think twice before drinking water," Caleb warns everyone. "We have to make our supply last until we get to another source."

You try to follow orders, but by the second day, it's really hard. The desert is drier and hotter than anyone expected, and it is making you extra thirsty. Plus you can't stop coughing. As the oxen plod along, they kick up so much dust it creates a big brown cloud, making it hard to breathe.

"We can't continue like this," Pa says. "We need to make it easier to travel somehow."

Caleb agrees. "We could travel by night and then rest during the day. The hot sun will be less of a problem that way. Or we could line up our wagons side to side instead of in a line," he suggests.

"What is the advantage of that?" Ma asks.

"That way you won't walk through the dust of the wagons in front of you," he says.

What do you do?

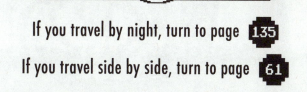

If you travel by night, turn to page **135**

If you travel side by side, turn to page **61**

Pa, the dogs didn't know that Gertie wasn't just a regular antelope," you say. "I would feel bad taking anything from them."

"I agree with you," Pa says, looking at you proudly. "I'll tell them what you said."

Pa goes back to the men and speaks to them. They nod their heads, then jump up on their horses and ride away. But just after you start to hike again, they return.

"We will travel with you as far as the next village," they say. One of the men smiles warmly at you. You learn that his name is Roaring Cloud and his son is Bright Sky. They are part of the Lakota Nation.

The next day, the men accompany your wagon train. Along the way, they point out various plants and tell you what is edible and what they use for making medicines. Ma listens carefully and makes notes in her journal.

Everyone is grateful to have the company of people so familiar with the land. It makes you feel safer. When you make camp, the Lakota disappear, and you wonder if they have left to go back to their homes. But then they come back, just as quickly as they left, and hand Ma a jackrabbit to add to supper. Ma prepares it into a savory stew that everyone shares. And as you sit around the campfire after a satisfying meal, Roaring Cloud tells you stories of his family and Lakota legends.

"Once upon a time, when the world was young, Porcupine had no quills," he starts.

"Really?" Hannah asks, her eyes huge as she listens intently.

"Porcupines were smooth like mice," Roaring Cloud continues, explaining how Porcupine, an animal who lived long ago, discovered prickly thorns from a bush. Porcupine put them on like a coat, then curled himself into a ball to keep Bear and Wolf away.

"Wow," Samuel says, enjoying the story as much as you are. You notice how your new friend's dark eyes shine in the light of the fire and wish that he and Bright Sky would stay with you all the way until Oregon.

The next day you arrive at the Lakota settlement, and your wagon train makes camp nearby. Roaring Cloud invites you to supper for a feast. You, Hannah, and Samuel gather a bunch of wildflowers to take with you. Pa brings some fuel that he's collected for the fire, too.

"This is so exciting!" Hannah

says, smoothing her apron over her dress. Even though it feels like a celebration, you don't have anything fancy to wear. You're still in the dusty dirty clothes you wear on the Trail. You all help Ma wash the clothes by the rivers as often as you can, but it's a process that takes hours. And your clothes get dirty again so quickly anyway.

The settlement is bustling with people coming in and out of the teepees. But one area is set up for the feast. Roaring Cloud greets you with a warm smile and offers you a seat in front of a mat that is covered with plates of food. A woman dressed in elaborate skins smiles at you, and you wonder if she is his wife.

"What's that?" Samuel asks, wrinkling his nose at the sight of the food.

"I don't know," you reply. "But it doesn't look like anything we've ever eaten before."

There is a loaf of bear root bread and wild onion stew and a cake-like thing made out of another kind of root. Pa has eaten the cake in the past, and says it tastes like a sweet potato. But you're not sure about any of this food.

You feel Roaring Cloud looking at you, and wonder if he notices that you aren't eating. You don't want to hurt his feelings, but you are not used to this kind of food. Do you force yourself to eat it? Or do you wait until you get back to your camp and have something safe and familiar, like the leftover beans from last night's supper?

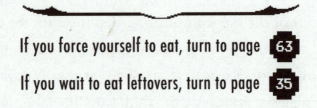

If you force yourself to eat, turn to page **63**

If you wait to eat leftovers, turn to page **35**

You don't want to wake Caleb so you rummage through the medicine chest for the tonic. It's too dark to search for a spoon, so you take a few gulps straight from the bottle. Then you get back to your tent and lie down again.

After a little tossing and turning you finally fall asleep. Soon you are in a heavy slumber and have weird dreams. In one dream, you have taken too much medicine and ended up poisoning yourself. Or is that your fate?

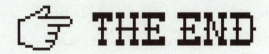 **THE END**

I think we should get off the Trail," you whisper to Pa.

"I think you're right," he replies. "If we don't find some food for the oxen soon, they won't make it much longer."

Luckily, everyone else finally agrees with you. You're feeling hopeful that conditions are going to get better as you veer south off the Trail. But after you travel for several miles, the terrain hasn't changed much, and you start to worry about whether or not you'll really find more grass or water on this path.

The wagon train stops for the midday break. Everyone starts snacking, but you can't stand not knowing what's ahead.

"Pa, I'm going to climb up that rock to see what's nearby," you say.

"Okay, but hurry," Pa says. "We have to get moving again soon."

You scramble to the top of the rock, which gives you a better view. A deep sense of disappointment washes over you as you stand at the top. As far as you can see, there is nothing but barren land.

Pa looks up at you and motions that it's time to leave. You slide down the rock and hurry back to your wagon. You shake your head at Pa without saying a word. He nods sadly, understanding.

Five days later, the oxen are weak and frail and you have not had a warm meal in days. It's just too difficult to find fuel for fires. You set up camp for the evening, and Ma tries to lift everyone's spirits by spreading the little bit of the molasses she has left on prairie biscuits, as a treat. You lick the sticky sweetness off your fingers, and are feeling a bit better when suddenly you hear the sound of hooves approaching. Is it Native American people, or maybe someone else who can help you? You've heard of groups of people who have made a business of helping weary pioneers.

"Do you think they are bringing us supplies?" you ask Pa.

"I'm not sure," Pa responds with a concerned look.

In the end, the riders don't bring you anything but trouble. They are bandits looking for lost and helpless victims like you. They rob you of everything valuable, including what's left of your money.

After they ride away, you hear nothing but stifled sobs. Now you are left with even less than you had before, stranded in a harsh and unwelcoming land. As your oxen start to die, you realize that you won't ever make it to Oregon.

☞ THE END

You scrap the idea of rummaging through the medicine chest without anyone to tell you what to take. But soon you see Ma peeking through your tent to check on you.

"How long have you been coughing like that?" she asks, concerned.

You shrug weakly. Ma returns a few minutes later with some medicine and an extra blanket.

"Here, take this and wrap yourself in this blanket," she says.

You drink the bitter tonic. And soon, under the weight of the blanket, you fall into a deep sleep.

Your wagon train is making its way along the Snake River. You've recovered from your cough and are feeling much better. That's a relief, because sometimes coughs are the start of deadly illnesses. Suddenly you hear the loud rushing of water.

"Those must be the Shoshone Falls," Caleb says,

listening carefully. "I've read they're supposed to be very impressive."

"Can we go see them?" Eliza asks. She's always on the lookout for an adventure.

"We can, if everyone doesn't mind extra hiking."

"I hear the falls are one of the wonders of the Trail," Ma says. "I'd like to see them."

Everyone else is equally eager so you agree to make the trek. When you reach the falls, they are one of the most beautiful sights you have ever seen. The rushing sheets of water drop down, foaming and frothing, from the cliffs above. The force of the water is so loud it can be heard from miles away.

A couple days later you come upon another amazing sight along the river. It's an area between two rapids where dozens of Shoshone people are spearing massive fish. You recognize the pinkish fish as the kind you tried for the first time at Fort Hall.

"Pa, look! It's salmon!" you say. "Can we get some?"

"Let's ask," Pa says, looking hungrily at the fish. You've had nothing but bacon and cornmeal pudding for days, and you could all use a change.

Pa barters for several large fish, which he grills over the campfire that night. Ma pulls out some potatoes that she has saved for a long time, and you all enjoy a delicious and satisfying supper.

The feast brings out the celebratory mood in everyone. After everyone is done eating, fiddles and harmonicas fill the air with song. You, Eliza, and Joseph play a game of cards. Samuel and Hannah entertain themselves by stringing together colorful beads that Ma got from the Shoshone people.

The evening gives everyone a nice break, which is important because of the big challenge ahead. You are about to approach Three Island Crossing, which is the hardest part of the Snake River to cross.

"Even though it's difficult, we need to cross the river here to avoid a rough desert route that would take us through massive sand dunes," Caleb explains.

"What is the crossing like?" Pa asks.

"First we have to ford one section of the river, which is about a hundred yards wide, to an island," Caleb says. "Then we cross a swift and dangerous branch to another island, and then there's one more part of the river to get across."

Everyone starts to talk about the best way to get across the river.

"I've heard we should tie the wagons together," one man suggests. "The extra weight makes it less likely that the wagons will tip over or drift downstream."

"Yes, but that is a lot of weight for the oxen," another man argues. "It might be better to take apart the wagons and float them across the river. That way the animals only have to manage themselves."

A discussion ensues about how to float the wagons and whether or not that is a better idea than connecting them together.

"It's up to you all," Caleb decides. "Whatever everyone agrees to do, we'll do."

A lively debate erupts until you come to your decision. What do you do?

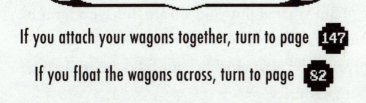

If you attach your wagons together, turn to page **147**

If you float the wagons across, turn to page **82**

The California Trail sounds like a better choice," Pa says to your family privately.

"I'm glad you think so," Ma says. "It also sounds safer to me."

"But what about your dream to have a farm in Oregon Territory?" you can't help but ask. You're surprised by how quickly your folks are ready to change course.

"If California doesn't work out the way we hope, we can still make the trip up the coast," Pa says. "And if there is as much gold as we are hearing about, we'll have all the money we need."

You guess he's right. Why not try out California first, especially if it's an easier trail?

But not everyone else agrees with you. More than half of your wagon train, including Caleb and his family, plans to continue on to Oregon. Three other wagons are joining you, splitting off from the rest. But you'll join up with another wagon train that is heading southwest from Fort Hall, too. That way, you'll have a larger group of fifteen wagons.

You don't think about how hard it will be to say goodbye to Joseph and Eliza until you reach the Raft River Crossing. There it finally hits you. They've been with you on the Trail since the very beginning, and have been wonderful friends. You hold back tears as you say goodbye, but Eliza sobs and holds you tight. Joseph blinks hard and gives you a half hug. When the Trail forks, you keep walking in the other direction.

"It looks like there are some nice people in this wagon train," Ma says, putting her arm around you. She's also sad to be leaving friends behind. You nod, trying to lift the heaviness off your heart.

The trail to California starts off pretty well. For several days you make good time, traveling at least twelve miles a day. But once you pass the Humboldt River, things quickly change. The land grows increasingly desolate and difficult to cross. There is almost no grass, the water tastes bad, and there's very little fuel. But your new wagon train captain, a rough man named Edward, is determined to push ahead.

"It has to get better," he insists.

"What are we going to do?" one man complains. "The animals are getting weaker and we are running out of feed."

"And I can't manage to get a decent campfire going," a woman adds. "We haven't had a proper hot meal for two days."

Everyone is tired, hungry, and frustrated. Soon the discussion turns into a shouting match. Some people agree with Edward, saying that you have no choice but to continue on the trail and wait for conditions to improve.

"If we change course now, it could get even worse," they argue.

Others are convinced that you need to veer off the trail to search for better grass and fuel.

"If it doesn't get better soon, we won't be able to continue," they say.

Ma gets everyone to calm down and talk to each other. What do you agree to do?

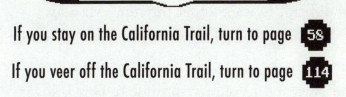

If you stay on the California Trail, turn to page **58**

If you veer off the California Trail, turn to page **114**

Heading south to Fort Bridger seems like the safest option. Your family tells the group you think they should take this route, even though it will take a bit longer. Everyone agrees.

You're relieved. The cutoff would have taken you through the desert. That evening, when the wagons stop for the night, your parents tell you stories they've heard about the desert.

"Some say the oxen drop from thirst," Pa says. "Some families lose their entire teams!"

"And people have to travel at night because it is too difficult to walk under the sun," Ma adds.

You imagine walking the dusty hot trail at night, using only the light of lanterns to guide you. You're glad everyone agreed to continue to Fort Bridger. Forts are welcome spots along the Trail for making wagon repairs, trading goods, and resting. And you especially like meeting kids from other wagon trains.

While your family sets up camp, you walk with Joseph to collect sagebrush for your campfire. Grass is scarce in this area, known as Little Sandy Crossing, and there isn't much fuel.

"Do you ever miss school?" Joseph asks you as you hike together.

"Sometimes," you reply, surprised at yourself. When you first learned you were going on the Trail, you were excited that you wouldn't have to go to school. Now you like it when Pa gives you lessons in geography or grammar and Ma quizzes you in sums and organizes the kids into spelling bees.

"Do you?" you ask Joseph.

"I do, a lot," Joseph says, as you expect. Joseph seems to know a little bit about almost everything.

"I miss books the most," he adds with a sigh. "I've read every book we have at least three times!"

As you head back with armfuls of brush, you point to smoke from another wagon train's camp. Like yours, they have grouped their wagons into a circle, or "corral." This keeps animals safe from wolves, coyotes, thieves, and from wandering away.

"Looks like we have even more company," Joseph

says, pointing to wisps of smoke in another direction. "That's a Native American settlement. The Shoshone are in these parts."

The fuel you bring back is enough to get a decent-size fire going, which Ma uses to cook your supper. You eat baked beans, with a little bit of bacon for seasoning, and some pan bread. At bedtime, you pull out your worn copy of *Gulliver's Travels*. But before you've read three pages, you're nodding off.

You wake up to a guard shouting an alarm.

"We've been robbed!" you hear. "A cow and two horses are missing!"

Thieves! Someone managed to sneak past your guard and steal the animals. It's barely light outside, and you realize it's very early in the morning.

Joseph beckons you over to his campsite.

"One of those groups we saw last night must have robbed us," he whispers. "I'm going to go spy on them. Cover for me if anyone asks."

Joseph takes off before you can protest.

After Joseph leaves, you wonder if you should tell Ma and Pa where he went, or go after him yourself. You don't want him to get angry with you for being a tattletale. But you don't want him to be out there alone, either. What do you do?

If you tell Pa what Joseph is doing, turn to page 70

If you go after Joseph, turn to page 39

Here you go, drink this," Pa says, adding a few drops of citric acid into your water-skin.

"What will that do?" you ask.

"I'm afraid you have scurvy," Pa says, with a worried frown. "We haven't had enough fruit or vegetables in our diet."

You've heard of scurvy before. It's a pretty serious ailment and it can even kill people. Thinking back on all the bacon, beans, and cornbread you've been eating, you're not surprised. You can't even remember the last time you had some fresh fruit. It must have been the wild berries someone collected weeks ago.

Even though you don't feel like eating or drinking anything, you force yourself to sip the water. Slowly, you start to feel a little better, and over the next few days your strength returns. But once you're feeling better, Hannah and Samuel start complaining of the same symptoms you had.

Pa orders everyone to drink the citric acid mix, but you've run out.

"I don't know what to do," Ma says. "If only we had brought along more of that veggie cake!"

You think back to the brown brick-like cake that the shopkeeper had showed you all the way back in Missouri, at the start of the Trail. It was made out of dried vegetables that were pressed into a giant block. At the time, you and Samuel wrinkled your noses at it because it looked like something animals would eat. But every now and then over the first month of your journey, Ma had broken off a piece and mixed it into the beans or rice she cooked.

"We don't have much of a choice," Pa says. "We have to push on to Fort Bridger. Let's just hope they have supplies of citric acid or fresh lemons there. We'll have to pick up what we can and get our strength back. Keep your eyes open for berries."

The fort is still several days away. You hope

everyone can make it that far. Hannah and Samuel are already having trouble walking. Looking at their weak faces, you are really scared and doubtful. You never wished for the veggies you used to leave on your plate more than right now.

☞ **THE END**

You decide to cross the river and look at the water current and the tiny gravel path that lies ahead. The sound of the water rushing makes it hard to hear. Ma holds on to Hannah's hand and you keep a tight grip on Samuel's as you walk behind the wagon. Every so often you can feel the uneven ground beneath you give way a little bit, but you manage to take another step forward.

"We're halfway across," Pa shouts.

You lean your body to the side so you can see Pa, when suddenly your foot slips off the narrow path. You hear Ma scream as Samuel tumbles down with you, into the water. You let go of his hand and try to grab on to something, to keep from being swept away. But the undercurrent pulls you down. You feel yourself flailing, and you swallow huge gulps of water as you desperately try to regain your footing.

Just when you think it's hopeless, a hand grabs you and pulls you up.

"Can you breathe?" Joseph asks.

You nod yes. You start coughing as you get to your feet. You see Samuel is safe with Pa. Joseph guides you slowly along the rest of the path, and you make it across the river. Ma and Pa rush toward you and give you and Joseph big hugs. They're certain Joseph saved your life.

Over the next couple of days, you keep coughing. After a while, the coughing becomes uncontrollable and you can't catch your breath. Soon you're wheezing heavily and have to lie down in the wagon. It hurts to cough, as if someone is squeezing your lungs. It becomes difficult to breathe. You have water in your lungs and will die of pneumonia.

☞ **THE END**

You decide to travel by night through the hot dusty desert. That way the sun won't be beating down on you, making it more difficult to travel. Plus you've already used up more of your water supply than you should have at this point. It's been extremely hard on the oxen to have to pull the weight of the wagons, including the heavy barrels of water, in the blistering heat. Moving under the cover of darkness will be easier on them.

But once you all agree to the plan, you realize that traveling by night means that you won't be sleeping tonight. After a short evening rest and supper, you are going to start moving again and continue until tomorrow morning.

"What if I can't walk another step?" Hannah asks, worried by the idea.

"We can take turns resting in the wagon, so it isn't too hard on the oxen," Ma replies.

Sitting in the creaky wagon with all your stuff isn't very comfortable, especially when it rolls over bumps. But it beats hours of endless walking.

When it gets dark, you head back out on the Trail. You, Joseph, and Eliza hold lanterns to guide the way. It feels spooky to be moving in the darkness by the glow of the moon and the flickering lights.

"Look," Joseph says, pointing to the sky. It's so clear you can see the constellations. You try to identify the ones you know.

"There's the Big Dipper," you say. As soon as the words are out of your mouth, you imagine a ladle being lowered into a big pot of cold refreshing water. But it isn't anywhere near time for a water break, so

you push the thought out of your mind and look for other shapes in the sky.

After a couple of hours of walking, you've lost all interest in the stars and the adventure of moving by night. You want to curl up in your tent and sleep. Your legs are sore and you stumble. Your lips are so dry and parched, you can't help but keep licking them, even though that just makes them worse.

Finally it's your turn to rest in the wagon, but it seems like only a minute before you're walking again. You barely notice the sunrise, and can only think that you are more ready for sleep than you have ever been.

Later you go to sleep in your tent, but you wake up after a couple of hours. It's too hot to sleep. You're sweating. Everyone else is fast asleep, but you walk outside to see if you can catch a breeze.

Outside, you see something glimmering in the distance, reflecting in the daylight. It's a lake! You give a little shout and start to run toward it, before you realize that you should grab the water-skins and fill them up. Do you take the water-skins and fill them up yourself so you can surprise everyone when they wake up? Or do you wake up Eliza so she can help you carry more water back? She is always game for an adventure and you know she would be as excited as you. But you feel bad waking her. What do you do?

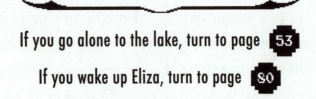

If you go alone to the lake, turn to page **53**

If you wake up Eliza, turn to page **80**

Everyone in your family agrees you must continue on the Oregon Trail. It's been Pa's dream for far too long to give it up, and now it's become all of yours, too. Even though the idea of gold sounds tempting, you've heard troubling stories of pioneers being disappointed and tricked by people leading them off the Trail.

Caleb's family is staying on the path to Oregon, which is a huge relief. Not only would it be hard to manage without Caleb as captain, but you also can't imagine the Trail without Joseph and Eliza. In the end, only three wagons decide to split off from the train. You'll be sorry to see them go.

After leaving Fort Hall, you hike for three days through sage-filled plains to the Raft River, which is a deep and rapid stream leading to the Snake River. It's also where the families leaving for California will finally turn southwest. The hike is pretty straightforward, except that it starts to rain hard on the second day and doesn't stop until the third. You trudge through the mud, soaking wet and cold.

When you get to the Raft River crossing, you and the other families who have stayed with the wagon train ford the stream easily. But soon after you get to the other side, you are startled when Joseph nudges you and nods toward the right.

There lies a gravestone that reads: "To the Memory of Lydia Edmonson, who died Aug. 16, 1847, Aged 25 years."

Your heartbeat quickens and a feeling of dread settles over you. So many pioneers don't get the choice of whether to go to Oregon or California.

"What are you looking at?" Hannah asks.

"Oh, nothing at all. We saw a funny bird," you reply, pointing in the other direction. "Look, did it fly over there?"

You feel guilty for fibbing, but you don't want your little sister to get scared. You think she might understand what graves are, but you don't ever talk about them in front of her, even on the bad days when you pass several. Luckily, Hannah is soon happily pointing out all the birds she sees and asking you if they are like the one you saw.

That evening your wagon train searches for a spot to make camp near the Snake River, which is rushing and hitting the rocks along the banks. Its water levels are higher than usual because of all the rain that's fallen over the past two days. Your scout picks out a spot, but the ground is muddy and soaked, and some of the others start to complain.

"This isn't a good spot to camp," one man says.

"It's too wet. Let's go find some higher ground," says another.

But looking for another spot means more walking and you, like many others, are tired.

"This is good enough," a woman argues. "I don't want to walk another step."

"Yes, it's fine. It's going to be wet everywhere," someone else agrees.

Ma and Pa look around at the area, uncertain. Then they look at you kids and see how tired you are.

"Do you want to make camp here, or keep looking for something better?" Ma asks you.

If you say you want to make camp here,
turn to page **48**

If you say you want to keep looking for something
better, turn to page **43**

You remember that a snake rattles its tail as a warning that it might strike. Even though your instincts tell you to spring off your mat and run away, you force yourself to lie still. You hold your breath, slowly counting the seconds in your head.

Archie doesn't move, either, although he looks poised to pounce on the snake. You desperately hope he doesn't.

After what feels like hours, but is probably only a few seconds, the brown spotted snake slithers into a small hole on the other side of the wooden hut.

"WOOF!" Archie runs after it and starts to bark at the hole, as if he is challenging the snake.

"Come here, boy," you say, in a shaky voice.

"What's going on?" Samuel asks in a whisper, his voice heavy with sleep.

"A snake," you say.

"Snake!" Hannah screams, waking up Ma and Pa. Everyone crowds around you as you tell them about your close encounter.

"Good thing you didn't try to strike it or run," Pa says. "Those snakes are deadly."

No one gets much more sleep that night, especially you. You keep checking to see if anything is coming near you. When the morning bugle sounds, you're still exhausted, even though you're not sorry at all to leave Fort Bridger.

★ ★ ★

You've entered Bear Lake Valley, a beautiful area with rolling hills and cedar groves. It's filled with plenty of firewood and water.

But Caleb has warned you all about the next obstacle ahead: the Big Hill. It's one of the steepest climbs on the Trail. After five days of hiking, you finally reach the point where you have to trek up the massive hill. Everyone stares at it in disbelief.

"Even if we get up that thing, how are we going to get down the other side?" Pa asks.

"One thing at a time," Caleb says. "We can do it if we're careful."

"I think we should use a windlass to get the wagons up," Joseph suggests.

"What's that?" you ask. You've never heard of one of those before.

"You anchor one wagon at the top of the hill, and attach ropes to its wheels," he says, getting excited by the possibility.

"Then what happens?"

"You attach the other end of the ropes to the rest of the wagons at the bottom of the hill. Then you turn the wheel on the windlass like a crank. It pulls the wagons up the hill."

"I've heard of windlasses being used successfully on the Trail," another man agrees. "We should try it."

If you use the windlass, the oxen would just have to get themselves up the hill, without carrying the weight of the wagons. But some of the others aren't so sure that it's a good idea. They're nervous about using something they aren't familiar with for the first time.

"What if it breaks?" someone says. "Or if it isn't strong enough?"

They think going slow and steady up the hill might be the best option, even if it would be challenging for the animals.

What do you decide?

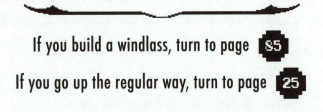

If you build a windlass, turn to page **85**

If you go up the regular way, turn to page **25**

You decide to tie two wagons together and cross the river in pairs. With double the weight, the wagons should be less likely to tip over in the strong current. Besides, the idea of disassembling your wagons and floating the parts across the river sounds like too much work. And there's too much potential for accidents or losing things in the process.

Your wagon is connected to Caleb's with heavy ropes. Soon everyone is ready to go.

"Let's roll the wagons," Caleb orders. "Move them slow and steady. And don't stop in the riverbed, just in case there is quicksand."

The first pair of wagons rolls into the water, and then the second follows. Yours are next. Ma is riding in your wagon with Hannah and Samuel because she isn't a very good swimmer and the water is too rough for her to walk in. You help Pa and Caleb lead the animals, along with Joseph and Eliza.

You step into the brisk water, which reaches up to your waist, ready for the first part of the crossing. You shiver and your teeth start to chatter. Archie jumps in after you and paddles happily.

"You have that thick warm coat, Archie," you grumble enviously.

The other animals are reluctant to get into the water, and you don't blame them. You wonder if it's because they don't want to be cold or because of how strong the current is.

"*Hiyaa!*" Pa calls, pulling them by their yokes. "Come on."

Finally, the oxen take the plunge. Slowly they make their way across the river as you lead them with ropes. Things are going smoothly until suddenly the wagons jerk violently.

SPLASH!

Something has fallen out of one of the wagons.

"Ma!" Hannah screams.

You see your mother's bonnet bobbing in the current, but you don't see the rest of her anywhere. Where is she?

Pa throws you his ropes. "Hold them steady!" he shouts. And then he dives after Ma.

You remember Caleb's warning about stopping in the river, so you keep your oxen moving. But you feel a lump in your throat and you want to cry out for Ma. What if she drowns?

Finally you see Pa swimming back, dragging Ma along behind him. She isn't moving, and he lifts her into the wagon. Then he jumps in and starts to press on her chest and blow into her mouth. As Pa keeps going, your heart pounds so hard it feels like it is going to rip out of your chest. It seems like time freezes until you finally hear a little cough and cry out with relief.

"She's alive!"

Pa gently sits Ma up. She has a cut on her head

that is bleeding and she looks confused, but other than that, she seems okay. Ma hit a rock when she fell out of the wagon. It knocked her unconscious, and she would have drowned if Pa hadn't acted so quickly.

"Can you handle the oxen?" Pa asks, as he dresses Ma's wound.

"Yes," you say, glad that there's something you can do to help.

"Let's keep moving," Caleb says, his face filled with emotion. "That was a close one."

You reach the island safely and take a rest before continuing on to the next crossing. Looking at the second island, you shudder, realizing that you will have to do this all over again.

Pa takes the ropes again and leads the oxen during the second stretch of the crossing. He looks at you from time to time and gives you an encouraging nod. You expertly steer the oxen with Caleb, and before too long, you make it to the other side of the river.

"We did it together," Pa says, smiling at you proudly. You smile back at Pa, and look at the rest of

your family, realizing how grateful you are for every one of them.

You've overcome so many obstacles on this journey so far, and each time you feel even closer to the people who survived them with you. Three Island Crossing is behind you now. Since you left Devil's Gate, you've had plenty of adventures and challenges, from rattlesnakes to the Big Hill. You've had good times with friends like Eliza and Joseph and made new friends like Roaring Cloud. You've tasted foods like Pacific salmon and even drank soda water from the ground!

It's been almost half a year since you left your

home in Kentucky and headed to Missouri to start the journey out West. Your old life seems like a distant memory, and all you know now is life on the Trail, with all its hardships and joys. But you are almost three-quarters of the way to Oregon City.

In the weeks ahead you will have to cross rugged mountains. Luckily your family has made good time since you started out on the Trail in May, so you won't still be trekking in the heart of winter. Even so, you know that the next part of the Trail will be the most difficult. But you're not worried. You've gotten this far, and you're ready for whatever is next. Because you are a tried-and-true pioneer!

☞ **THE END**

Three Island Pass

AUGUST 24, 1850

GUIDE
to the Trail

GET READY TO EXPLORE!

You have completed half of the Oregon Trail, pioneer! You've relied on your wits, good judgment, and resources like this travel guide to get this far. Making it through the rest of the journey requires you to stay alert and to watch out for dangers, from wild animals and harsh climates to swindlers looking to profit off of you. The next part of the Trail also involves difficult decisions on how best to navigate, so be careful and choose wisely.

DANGERS!

FLASH FLOODS

Floods can wipe out entire camps, if you aren't careful to make camp in the right spot. Avoid sites next to rivers with overflowing banks and damp ground.

SNAKEBITE

Snakebites are common on the Trail and can be deadly if the snake is venomous. If you encounter a rattlesnake, do not make sudden movements or strike it. If it rattles, it is scared. Stay as still as possible and it will probably leave you alone.

DISEASE

Staying healthy on the Trail can be difficult. Eat the cleanest and freshest foods you can in order to avoid dysentery. If you get diarrhea, drink water mixed with salt and sugar. Another serious condition is scurvy, which is the result of not eating enough fruit and vegetables. Symptoms include weakness, paralysis, bleeding gums, and loss of teeth. The condition can be reversed by eating citrus fruits or citric acid.

HEAT

If you find yourself in desert-like conditions on the Trail, it is safest to travel by night. Stock up on water and ration it carefully. Watch out for signs of heat stroke or exhaustion, such as rapid breathing, nausea, and headaches in yourself and others. You can hallucinate if you are dehydrated, so if you see something strange, ask a friend if they see it, too.

FOREST FIRES

A real threat on the mountains, forest fires are swift and deadly. You may not be able to safely outrun a fire, but climbing out of its reach is an option.

POISONING

Avoid buying any medicine, called "tonic" on the Trail, from people you don't trust or know. When you feel sick, always check with an adult for the right amount of medicine, so you do not poison yourself or fall ill from accidentally taking too much.

👉 FINDING YOUR WAY

Walking 2,000 miles (3,200 km) from Missouri to Oregon City in 1850 means there aren't roads or many signs. You have to navigate by landmarks along the way.

SOUTH PASS

This gently sloping pass marks the halfway point on the Oregon Trail and the location of the Continental Divide.

GREENWOOD CUTOFF

This shortcut saves a week of travel, but takes you through a scorching desert. The longer trip is advisable but the longer you are on the trail, the more risks you potentially face.

GREEN RIVER

This is one of the most dangerous river crossings on the Trail. Take the ferry instead of fording the river.

BIG HILL

Big Hill is one of the steepest hills on the Trail. A windlass, which allows you to mechanically crank up wagons without straining your animals, may be a good option. But a windlass has risks of its own.

SODA SPRINGS

A marvel of the Trail, Soda Springs is a fascinating place filled with naturally bubbling pools of carbonated water. Be careful though; some of the hot springs are extremely hot and can cause you serious burns!

SHOSHONE FALLS

You can hear these impressive and spectacular waterfalls from miles away.

THREE ISLAND CROSSING

This path across the Snake River involves strong currents and high waters. One option is to float your wagon across piece by piece, but that is a risky and often disastrous undertaking.

Look for these landmarks between Devil's Gate and Three Island Pass

DISTANCE FROM INDEPENDENCE, MISSOURI:

SOUTH PASS: 914 miles (1,471 km)

FORT BRIDGER: 1,026 miles (1,651 km)

SODA SPRINGS: 1,155 miles (1,859 km)

FORT HALL: 1,217 miles (1,959 km)

SHOSHONE FALLS: 1,337 miles (2,152 km)

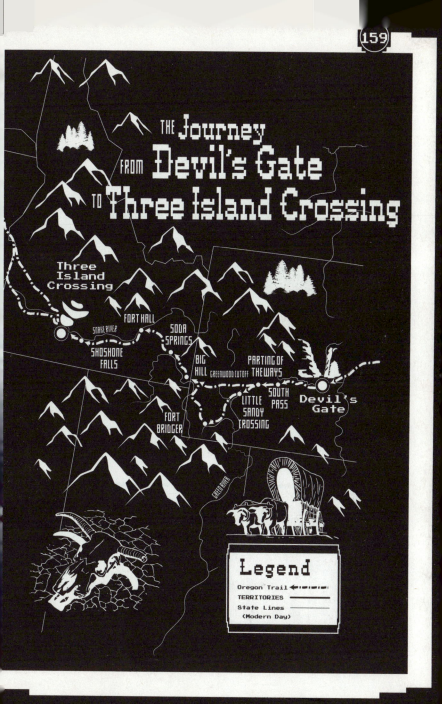

THE Journey FROM **Devil's Gate** TO **Three Island Crossing**

Three Island Crossing

FORT HALL

SNAKE RIVER

SODA SPRINGS

SHOSHONE FALLS

BIG HILL

GREENWOOD CUTOFF

PARTING OF THE WAYS

SOUTH PASS

LITTLE SANDY CROSSING

Devil's Gate

FORT BRIDGER

GREEN RIVER

Legend

Oregon Trail

TERRITORIES

State Lines
(Modern Day)

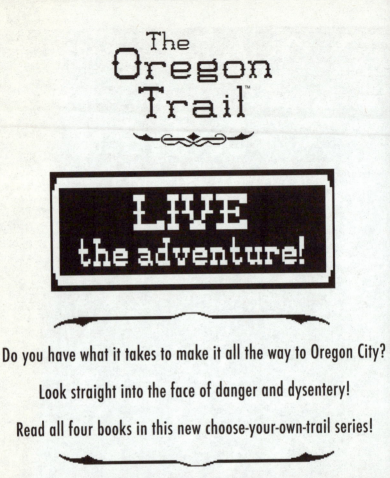